MOBY SHINOBI

NINJA AT THE FIREHOUSE

by Luke Flowers

SCHOLASTIC INC.

FOR MY SON, OWEN.

May you always face life's challenges with bravery and overcome them with the character of a "Titan." Thank you for the joyful laughter and wacky zest for life you bring to all of our adventures. I'm proud to be your pa!

Library of Congress Cataloging-in-Publication Data

Names: Flowers, Luke, author, illustrator. | Flowers, Luke. Moby Shinobi.
Title: Ninja at the firehouse / by Luke Flowers.
Description: New York, NY : Scholastic Inc., 2018. | Series: Moby Shinobi |
Summary: Told in rhyme, Moby puts his ninja skills to work "helping" at the local firehouse, but he ends up making more work for the firefighters—but his skills do come in handy when a cat needs rescuing.
Identifiers: LCCN 2018009412| ISBN 9781338256116 (pbk.) | ISBN 9781338256123 (hardcover)
Subjects: LCSH: Ninja—Juvenile fiction. | Fire stations—Juvenile fiction. | Helping behavior—Juvenile fiction. | Animal rescue—Juvenile fiction. | Stories in rhyme. | Humorous stories. | CYAC: Stories in rhyme. Ninja—Fiction. | Fire departments—Fiction. | Helpfulness—Fiction. | Humorous stories. | LCGFT: Humorous fiction. | Stories in rhyme. Classification: LCC PZ8.3.F672 Ng 2018 | DDC [E]—dc23 LC record available at https://lccn.loc.gov/2018009412

10 9 8 7 6 5 4 3 2 1   18 19 20 21 22

Printed in the U.S.A.   40
First printing 2018
Book design by Steve Ponzo

3

Stuff! Twist! Stack! I use ninja might.

Rake! Swing! Soar! Watch as I take flight.

Toss! Run! Climb! There is one last leaf.

Moby thinks of his ninja bin.
He grabs an armful to begin.

SWING!

STUFF!

14

Moby thinks of a water fight.
He holds the big hose ninja tight.

Dee Dee is teaching ladder skills.
She needs a helper for the drills.

20

**Moby thinks of a ninja run.
He must race to get this job done!**

RUN!

STICK!

24

RING! Smoke and fire fill the air!
The firefighters all rush there.

Moby thinks of big ninja flips.
He grabs a hose and off he zips!